THE LAST PRIME

Transformers: Revenge of The Fallen: The Last Prime

TRANSFORMERS, the logo, and all related characters are trademarks of Hasbro and are used with permission.

© 2009 Hasbro. All Rights Reserved.

© 2009 DreamWorks, LLC and Paramount Pictures Corporation. All Rights Reserved.

HarperCollins®, ♣®, and HarperEntertainment™ are trademarks of HarperCollins Publishers.

Printed in the United States of America.

No part of this book may be used or reproduced in any manner whatsoever without written permission except in the case of brief quotations embodied in critical articles and reviews. For information address HarperCollins Children's Books, a division of HarperCollins Publishers, 10 East 53rd Street, New York, NY 10022.

www.harpercollinschildrens.com

Library of Congress catalog card number: 2008940052

ISBN 978-0-06-172972-0

Book design by John Sazaklis

09 10 11 12 13 LP/CW 10 9 8 7 6 5 4 3 2

❖

First Edition

TRANSFORMERS

REVENGE OF THE FALLEN

THE LAST PRIME

Adapted by Tracey West

Based on the Screenplay by

Ehren Kruger & Alex Kurtzman & Roberto Orci

HarperEntertainment

An Imprint of HarperCollinsPublishers

PROLOGUE

IN THE BEGINNING, THE ALLSPARK ENERGY SOURCE brought life to the planet Cybertron by creating the thirteen Primes—the first Transformers.

But more energy was needed. So the Primes created the Matrix of Leadership, which supplied power to a huge machine that could extract the energy from suns. The Primes roamed the universe seeking suns that could be mined for energy. They had one rule: No sun would be destroyed if it gave life to the worlds around it.

Earth was one planet the Transformers explored for energy. But early humans were starting to walk the Earth, and the one rule was invoked.

One of the Primes, known as The Fallen, did not follow this rule. Because he wanted the Matrix for himself, The Fallen waged war on his twelve brothers.

In order to protect the Matrix of Leadership, the twelve noble Primes sealed themselves and the Matrix inside a tomb somewhere on planet Earth. For thousands of years the tomb remained hidden while The Fallen waited, hovering in space.

Now The Fallen has returned—and the fate of Earth is uncertain. There is only one who can defeat him, only one who has inherited the responsibility. The last Prime.

Optimus Prime.

CHAPTER 1

ON THE OUTSKIRTS OF THE BUSY CITY OF SHANGHAI, China, a pink ice cream truck cruised down the backstreets. Two kids ran out onto the street after the truck, waving their money.

Suddenly a siren blared from the steelyard next door, and the ice cream truck abruptly turned on its back wheels and zoomed back up the street . . . right toward the children! The startled kids were frozen to the spot. At the last second, though, the truck split in two . . . and passed right around them! Then the two pieces came right back together. A stream of popsicles flowed out the back of the truck.

The ice cream truck raced to the steelyard, where a swarm of soldiers emerged from a black pickup truck. Each man wore a patch on his shoulder with a skull symbol and the word *N.E.S.T.*—which stood for Nonbiological Extraterrestrial Species Treaty. A global alliance had been formed to track down Decepticons. Helicopters circled overhead.

Strike Force leader Major William Lennox addressed his men. "All right, guys, let's rock!"

"Thought we were rollin' today," joked his friend, Master Sergeant Ray Epps.

Now empty of soldiers, the black pickup began to change. Gears groaned and creaked as the truck took the shape of a hulking robot made of black metal. Ironhide had a missile shooter on one arm and a cannonlike pulse weapon on the other.

"He's here," Ironhide said, sensing an enemy Decepticon.

The ice cream truck rolled up beside him, and Ironhide sighed.

"Twins, just try to stay out of trouble," he warned.

Ironhide followed the soldiers around the steelyard and surrounding construction site. The lot was mostly filled with big cement pipes, overgrown weeds, and a few old construction vehicles. Lennox used an Energon Tracker, which would beep if it detected any Decepticon energy. So far, the machine was quiet. Lennox scanned a stack of pipes.

Beep beep beep beep BEEP BEEP BEEP BEEP!

BAM! The cement pipes went flying, pushed aside by a big rig with a one-armed bucket loader. It quickly changed into a Decepticon with two massive wheels. The soldiers opened fire as the robot thundered forward, crushing everything in its path.

Lennox barked into his headset. "Air support, be advised!

Target is headed for the quarantine perimeter. Do not let it get past!"

The Decepticon, called Demolisher, raced down the highway toward the city. Overhead, a C-17 aircraft dipped low. Its loading bay opened up, and a blue semitruck with painted flames parachuted down. The truck quickly changed into a large blue robot, Optimus Prime.

Optimus slammed onto the highway, morphed back into a truck, and began chasing Demolisher. The Decepticon jumped off an overpass, balancing on one wheel. He flipped end over end on the two big wheels, crushing cars in his path.

Optimus drove onto the next overpass, waiting to strike.

SMASH! Demolisher crashed right into the overpass. Optimus switched to his robot form, and then jumped onto Demolisher's neck.

Just in time, the black pickup caught up. It turned into Ironhide and slid underneath Demolisher, grabbing onto one big wheel. Together, he and Optimus slammed Demolisher into the concrete. The steel monster shuddered and collapsed in a junk heap.

Optimus looked down at Demolisher.

"This is not your planet to rule," the Decepticon said weakly. "The Fallen . . . shall rise . . . again."

CHAPTER 2 ...

SAM WITWICKY PACED BACK AND FORTH IN FRONT OF his television, furious.

"... Today, two years after the destruction in Mission City, the Wyatt Commission presented Congress with its official findings," the TV reporter was saying. "The Commission places all responsibility with defense contractor McClaren Robotics and dismisses all other reports as media conspiracy theories."

"And people believe it!" Sam fumed. "This is so lame!"

Two years ago, Sam had been just a normal high school student. Then his whole life turned upside down when he helped Optimus Prime and the Autobots save the world from Megatron and the evil Decepticons. These days the Autobots lived on Earth, helping to protect the planet from Decepticons. But hardly anybody knew that secret. Sam and his girlfriend Mikaela knew. His mom and dad knew. So did the soldiers who worked with N.E.S.T.

Everyone else believed the lies.

"Let's go! Let's go! All hands and pants on deck!" yelled Sam's dad, Ron.

Sam's mom, Judy, smothered him in a hug. "I'm losing my baby!" she wailed. Then she burst into tears and ran out of the room.

"We're proud of you, kiddo," Ron said. "First Witwicky ever to go to college."

Sam's cell phone rang. The name *Mikaela* popped up on the screen. Sam nodded to his dad and answered the phone. He walked to his bedroom as he talked.

"I'm breaking up with you," Mikaela said. Sam was going to college all the way across the country. How were they supposed to stay together?

Sam had the answer. "I'm making you a long-distance relationship kit," he said. "Some poetry I wrote—not all of it rhymes, but it's from the heart. Some souvenirs from the-event-that-cannot-be-mentioned. How about my shirt? The infamous D-day shirt?"

"You kept your nasty shredded clothes?" Mikaela asked.

Sam pulled the shirt from his drawer. "You kidding? I bled in this shirt."

Mikaela sighed. Sam could always win her over. "I'll be over in twenty."

Sam opened up his ratty shirt, and a small, charred ember

fell into his hand. Sam gasped. It was a piece of the AllSpark!

The AllSpark was an alien cube, the energy source for all Transformers. Megatron wanted to control it. In the end, Sam had used it to destroy Megatron. It was extremely powerful.

Suddenly the AllSpark sliver sparked and began to burn with heat. Sam dropped it. It hit the floor and burned through the wood, falling down into the kitchen.

The ember bounced around the kitchen, animating every electrical appliance there. The toaster jumped off the counter. The cappuccino maker shot fireballs across the room. The garbage disposal smashed through the sink cabinet, flashing sharp blades. A cell phone on the counter began to twitch and chatter. The microwave grabbed it, shoved it inside its belly, and turned itself on, frying the phone.

Then the appliances marched upstairs into Sam's room and swarmed him.

"Hey!" Sam cried out as the electric mixer blasted him with a hail of tiny pellets. He scrambled out of his bedroom window and fell onto the awning over his back porch. From there he tumbled into some bushes.

The kitchen bots opened fire from Sam's window. Sam grabbed his mom and dad and ran to safety.

BOOM! The bots blew up the backyard doghouse.

"Bumblebee!" Sam yelled.

⋙ CHAPTER 3 ⋘

A YELLOW AND BLACK CAMARO SMASHED THROUGH Sam's garage wall. The car changed into Bumblebee, Sam's friend and guardian.

Bumblebee aimed the missile launcher on his right arm at the army of 'bots, then blasted a huge hole in the side of the house.

"My house!" Judy screamed.

Bumblebee went back into the garage just before firefighters arrived to put out the blaze. Sam ducked into the house and found the ember of the AllSpark on the kitchen floor. He tucked it into an empty film canister to keep it safe.

Mikaela rode up on her motorcycle. She took off her helmet, and her dark brown hair spilled over her shoulders.

"What happened?" she asked Sam, her blue eyes wide.

Sam slipped the canister into her hand. "Do me a favor and keep this sliver hidden, okay?" he asked. "Someplace safe."

Mikaela nodded and slipped it into her bag. Sam walked into the garage. Bumblebee waited for him there, looking guilty. He tried to talk, but only a garbled squeal came out. He couldn't talk like other Autobots, but he could use the radio to communicate.

"Listen, Bee," Sam said. "I wanted to talk to you about college. It's just that freshmen aren't allowed to have cars. It's a lame rule. Besides, you should be with the other Autobots. You have a bigger purpose, right?"

Bumblebee flipped through the radio dial until he found the words he needed. "What . . . is . . . *your* . . . purpose . . . Sam?"

"I don't know," Sam said. "Be normal. Go to college and figure out what I want. I gotta do that alone."

Bumblebee nodded sadly. Sam walked back outside. He had one more good-bye to say.

He grabbed Mikaela and hugged her. "We're gonna make this work. I promise," he told her.

They kissed, and Sam got into the car with his parents.

His new life was about to begin.

... CHAPTER 4 ...

INSIDE DIEGO GARCIA AIR BASE, LOCATED SOMEWHERE in the Indian Ocean, was the secret base of N.E.S.T.

Optimus Prime was debriefing the military about what had happened in Shanghai. Lennox and Epps were there, along with a visitor—National Security Advisor Theodore Galloway. Admiral Morshower joined them on a monitor.

Optimus played a recording of Demolisher's ominous message: "The Fallen . . . shall rise . . . again."

"'The Fallen'? Meaning what?" the admiral asked.

"We don't know, sir," Optimus replied. "The recorded history of our race was contained within the AllSpark—and lost with its destruction."

Theodore Galloway did not trust the Autobots at all.

"No one can tell me what the enemy is after," he said. "There's one clear conclusion. You. The Autobots. They are here to hunt you. Our planet isn't safe with you on it. If the president asks you to leave peacefully, in the interest of national security, will you do it?"

"If you make that request, we will honor it," Optimus said. "But before your president decides, ask him this: What if we leave . . . and you're wrong?"

Galloway didn't listen to Optimus's warning. But as he would soon find out, he should have.

That night, a Decepticon named Ravage broke into the base, where N.E.S.T. had hidden what they thought was the last remaining piece of the AllSpark. Its existence was top secret. But Ravage found it and stole it, rocketing off into the sky to take it back to the Decepticons.

...CHAPTER 5

SAM HAD COME TO COLLEGE TO ESCAPE HIS OLD LIFE. But it just wasn't working.

First there was his roommate, Leo, who unlike other humans actually believed in the Transformers. He even had a website about them.

Then there were the strange symbols that had popped into Sam's head ever since he'd touched that piece of the AllSpark. He couldn't stop thinking about the weird alien writing, and he didn't know what it meant.

He tried to go to a party to get the symbols out of his mind. But before he could have fun, Bumblebee drove up!

"What are you doing here?" Sam asked Bumblebee.

Bumblebee took Sam to an old graveyard on the edge of town. Sam got out of the car and saw Optimus Prime standing on a hill, bathed in moonlight.

"You won't even give me one day in college? Just one day?" Sam asked.

"Hello, Sam," Optimus said. "A fragment of the AllSpark was stolen. I am here for your help."

"My help? I thought you had things handled," Sam replied.

"Some of your leaders think we've brought vengeance upon your planet," Optimus said. "They must be reminded by a human of the trust we share. Speak for us. Stand with us, Sam."

"I just got here!" Sam said. "I worked my whole life for this. You're a forty-foot alien robot. If the government won't listen to you, they're sure not going to listen to me."

Optimus would not give up. "There is more to you than meets the—"

"Stop!" Sam blurted out angrily. "I can't help you! You'll be able to convince them. After all, you're Optimus Prime."

Sam turned and walked out of the graveyard, leaving the Autobots behind.

⫶⫶⫶ CHAPTER 6

DEEP IN THE WATERS OF THE NORTH ATLANTIC SEA, Ravage and three Constructicons made their way across the sea floor. The Constructicons shone a light on the remains of a huge Decepticon. His metal body was covered in moss and barnacles.

Megatron.

After Sam had destroyed him, soldiers had buried Megatron in the ocean depths. Now the Doctor, a spiderlike Decepticon with eyes like headlights, skittered around Megatron's body.

"Ravage! The Shard!" the Doctor commanded in the language of the Decepticons.

Ravage turned over the shard of the AllSpark that had been stolen from the military base. The Doctor carefully placed the shard inside a hole in Megatron's chest.

At first nothing happened.

Then, slowly, Megatron's body began to quiver. The shard began to shine with searing blue light. The Decepticons

watched as the broken pieces of Megatron's body fused together. A bright red light shone in Megatron's eyes.

The leader of the Decepticons rose from the sea floor and blasted toward the surface of the water. Then Megatron soared into the blue sky and beyond, traveling through space until he reached a distant, icy planet. Embedded in a rocky gorge on the planet's surface was a spaceship, the *Nemesis*.

Megatron stomped to the ship's bridge and stopped in front of a metal triangle on the floor. The face of The Fallen appeared before him.

Megatron had tried to steal the AllSpark so that The Fallen could bring his old army to life. But Sam had stopped him, and Megatron had failed. Now The Fallen wanted another energy source—the Matrix of Leadership.

"The AllSpark knew where the Matrix was hidden," The Fallen said. "Its power and knowledge were absorbed by the boy that bested you. You must find him. Then you will have what you have always sought. For you, too, will be a Prime."

The Fallen disappeared. Another Decepticon stepped forward out of the shadows behind Megatron.

"He spoke of the boy, Lord Megatron." Starscream's eyes gleamed. He was eager to please his master. "We are already watching him."

CHAPTER 7

SAM MIGHT HAVE BEEN TRYING TO LIVE A TRANSFORMER-free life, but he just couldn't get those alien symbols out of his head.

Sam knew this had happened once before. Years ago, his great-great-grandfather had discovered Megatron on an expedition to the Arctic. After that, Captain Archibald Witwicky had started writing strange symbols—the same symbols that Sam kept drawing!

He raced across campus, talking to Mikaela on his cell phone.

"Mikaela, listen, something's happening to me," he said. "It's like my brain's going haywire. It happened after I touched that cube splinter from the AllSpark. You still have it, right?"

"Yeah," Mikaela replied. She was working in her dad's auto shop. "The shard's right here in the shop safe."

"Do *not* touch it!" Sam warned.

Just then, Mikaela heard a noise. She turned to look.

Wheels, a Decepticon spy-drone, was trying to break into her safe! She quickly grabbed a pair of metal tongs and pinned the bot to the wall. With her left hand, she picked up a blowtorch.

"What are you doing here, you little freak?"

"Seek knowledge from AllSpark!" Wheels replied. "Any piece! Secrets of Dynasty must be reclaimed!"

"What secrets?" Mikaela asked.

"The Fallen commands!" Wheels cried. "Show mercy, Warrior Goddess! I'm merely a salvage-scrap surveillance drone."

"And I'm merely your worst nightmare," Mikaela told him. She got back on the phone with Sam. "I'm getting on a plane. Just be careful."

That night Sam stood on his bed, tracing the alien symbols on the walls with his finger, when someone knocked and came into his dorm room. It was Alice, the pretty girl who lived in the room across the hall.

"Sam, I knew there was something amazing about you," she said. "You're, like, a genius."

Alice grabbed Sam's hand and pushed him against the wall.

"What the—wow, you're strong!" Sam said.

Alice leaned in to kiss Sam. That's when Mikaela walked

in, carrying a metal box. Seeing Alice with her arms around Sam made her furious.

"Great!" she snapped. "Thanks a lot, Sam."

Mikaela turned to storm out. Alice's eyes gleamed. A long, spiked metal tongue shot out of her mouth. It wrapped around Sam's neck.

WHACK! She lifted Sam up and hurled him across the room. Alice was a Decepticon!

Mikaela heard the noise and turned back around, stunned. She hurled the metal box at Alice's head. It hit its target and then crashed through Sam's window. The robot's head spun around crazily.

Sam's roommate, Leo, raced in—then immediately turned and ran back out. Sam and Mikaela followed him. The Alice 'bot sent a barrage of sharp metal spikes flying toward them, but they closed the door just in time.

"It's a metal she-beast!" Leo yelled. "What the heck's happening, Witwicky?"

"She's an alien robot," Sam shouted back. "Move!"

⚡ CHAPTER 8 ⚡

SAM, ALICE, AND LEO RACED INTO THE PARKING LOT.
Mikaela found an open car, and they climbed inside. She quickly
hot-wired the car and started the engine. Sam grabbed the
metal box and jumped in the car with Leo. Then they zoomed
away from campus as fast as they could.

Leo was freaking out. "I want to hear all about this—where
they come from, what they're doing here," he told Sam.

"Here's how it is," Sam explained. "They blow up buses
like a bag of chips. They take down planes. And if you ever hear
one of them coming, it's already too la—"

WHAM! A massive Decepticon MH-53 helicopter had
dropped from the sky. A steel spike pierced the roof, and the
helicopter lifted the car into the air.

The chopper flew to an old steel foundry and dropped
the car straight through the building's roof. The car slammed
into the concrete, and Sam, Leo, and Mikaela stumbled out.

Starscream stood in front of Mikaela and Leo. Megatron loomed over Sam.

"Remember me?" Megatron asked. "I remember you."

Sam tried to run away, but Megatron swatted at him with one massive hand. Sam landed on a metal slab, and Megatron pinned him down.

"You will pray for a sudden death, insect," Megatron promised.

Sam noticed medical instruments on a table next to him. A microscope changed into the Doctor. He climbed onto Sam's chest with spidery metal legs. One of his arms turned into a hacksaw. He leaned over Sam's skull.

"You have something on your mind," Megatron said. "Something I need."

Suddenly the Doctor stopped. He noticed a small red laser dot on his chest.

BOOM! The Doctor exploded into pieces as Optimus Prime crashed through the foundry roof. He fired missiles at Megatron and Starscream from both of his arms. Bumblebee ran in and grabbed Mikaela and Leo.

Optimus grabbed Sam in one massive hand and charged outside. Megatron, in his jet form, opened fire. Optimus crashed through the forest, knocking down trees as he ran.

BOOM! One of Megatron's missiles hit Optimus, and the big Autobot fell, rolling down an embankment. Sam tumbled out of his hand.

"There is another AllSpark source on this planet," Megatron said, landing in robot form. "The boy can lead us to it. The Fallen has decreed it!"

Starscream flew onto the scene, switching from a jet to a robot as he landed next to Megatron. The MH-53 chopper joined them, changing into a hulking 'bot with whirring blades for arms. Optimus rose to his feet. Megatron charged.

"Run!" Optimus yelled to Sam. "Go now!"

Sam raced off as the three Decepticons descended on Optimus.

CHAPTER 9

SAM JUMPED INTO BUMBLEBEE WITH MIKAELA AND LEO. He had escaped Megatron—but not for long. Just hours later, Megatron appeared on television screens all around the world.

"Insects of the human hive: Now you know what your leaders have hidden from you. We are here. Among you," Megatron boomed.

People everywhere stopped and stared, shocked by what they saw.

"We can destroy your cities at will," Megatron announced. "If you wish them to remain standing, you will search for *this* boy."

The screen flashed, and the whole world saw Sam's face.

Megatron's threat was all Theodore Galloway needed to shut down N.E.S.T. He showed up at McGuire Air Force Base with an order from the president.

The Autobots had to stand down.

Bumblebee took Sam, Mikaela, and Leo to an old abandoned prison. The Twins showed up, no longer looking like two halves of an ice cream truck—they had changed into two Smart Cars, one orange and one green. They explained that the Autobots had been ordered by Galloway to stand down. Lennox and Epps were taking care of Optimus, who had been badly injured.

Sam realized that the symbols in his head were the key to everything. Leo thought he knew someone who might be able to help—a guy who called himself Robo-Warrior online. He had a website all about aliens, just like Leo did.

They traveled to Brooklyn to find Robo-Warrior and learned he was none other than Agent Simmons—although now he was just Simmons. Sam and Mikaela had run into him before, when the Transformers first came to Earth. Simmons had been working for the government back then. Now he was retired.

Simmons reluctantly agreed to help them. He told them the symbols had been around for a long time. He thought maybe a Decepticon would be able to read them.

Luckily Mikaela had brought a Decepticon along with her—Wheels. Bumblebee's trunk opened, and Mikaela took out the metal box. She opened it and picked up Wheels.

"Speak English," she ordered. "What do these mean?"

"Oh, language of the Primes!" Wheels said, excited. "I know not, but Seekers will tell you. Old Transformers. Old, old, old! Stranded, stuck. Thousands of years. I know where Seekers are!"

Wheels projected a map onto Simmons's wall. A red laser dot appeared on ten cities in the United States.

"Closest one's in Washington," Simmons said. "And I got news for you guys—we're going to need tickets."

⫸CHAPTER 10⫷

BUMBLEBEE AND THE TWINS TOOK THE FOUR HUMANS to Washington, D.C., to the Smithsonian Air and Space Museum. They waited until closing, and then Leo and Simmons tricked the guards so they could sneak inside.

Sam and Mikaela walked down the corridors of the museum. Old airplanes—some of the first ever made—were displayed behind velvet ropes. Mikaela gave Sam the film canister holding the small shard of the AllSpark. Sam held it up. If there was a Transformer in this museum, the shard would let him know.

Simmons and Leo followed as the group walked up and down the hallways. Suddenly the shard began to glow faintly. Then it jumped out of Sam's hand, magnetically drawn to an SR-71 Blackbird. The spy plane had a long, sleek body and a dull, black metal exterior.

The shard released a pulse blast, bathing the plane in blue light. The engine sputtered to life. Sam noticed a Decepticon symbol on the plane's door as it groaned and wheezed, changing before them into an old, rusty robot.

"Name's Jetfire, you bite-sized bipeds," the old Transformer snapped. "I'm on a mission. No time for chitchat. Behold me! Behold me and . . . something."

They followed Jetfire into a dusty hangar where old airplanes were stored. Sam tried to explain to Jetfire why they needed his help. Jetfire was confused. He told Sam that he had changed sides long ago in the war between the Decepticons and the Autobots. He had a mission now, but he just couldn't remember what it was.

"Listen," Sam said. "If you can help me, maybe I can help you."

Sam drew the alien symbols in the dust. Jetfire's eyes popped when he saw them. "I just keep writing them," Sam explained. "Whatever it means, Megatron wants it. He and someone called The Fallen."

"The Fallen!" he cried. "My boy, you may have saved us all! Now I remember what I was seeking. The Dagger's Tip! The Kings! And the key!"

Jetfire's chest plate opened up. The power source inside him burned bright blue. Blue forks of lightning fired out, swirling together to form a vortex of light and energy.

BOOM!

The black hole sucked them inside, one by one.

And one by one, it spit them out onto a vast expanse of sand.

"Here we are," Jetfire announced. "Egypt!"

⊷ CHAPTER 11 ⊷

SAM COULDN'T BELIEVE IT. "EGYPT?"

"Haven't opened up a trans-dimensional bridge in ages," Jetfire said. "Oh, my aching hull."

"Focus!" Sam said impatiently. "Why are we in Egypt?"

Jetfire led them to a rock bluff overlooking the desert. He projected an image from his chest: a daggerlike piece of metal with a crystal in its center.

"The Matrix of Leadership," Jetfire said. He told them how the Primes had created the Matrix and the machine that could destroy suns and collect their power. "Somewhere beneath the desert lie both the Matrix and the machine. The Fallen intends to return . . . to activate the machine."

"Then how do we defeat him?" Mikaela asked.

"Only a Prime can defeat him," Jetfire answered. "Only one survives, forever unaware of his destiny."

"Optimus Prime," Sam said softly. "He can't fight. He was injured . . . saving me."

Everyone was silent. Sam stared at the shard of the AllSpark in his hand. An idea formed.

"You said the Matrix could power that machine. Is there any way the energy of the Matrix could heal Optimus?" he asked.

Jetfire scratched his head. "You could be right!"

"Then how do we find the Matrix before the Decepticons find me?" Sam asked.

"All I can do is translate your symbols," Jetfire replied. "'When dawn alights the Dagger's Tip, Three Kings will reveal the doorway.'"

Then Jetfire sighed. "Alas, my friends, it'll be up to you from here. My weary wings may draw unwanted Decepticon attention."

Sam, Mikaela, Leo, and Simmons climbed into Bumblebee. The Twins followed them as they raced across the desert sand, searching for the location of the Matrix.

Simmons closed his cell phone. He already had a lead. "My CIA contact says ancient Sumerians used to call the Gulf of Aqaba 'the Dagger,'" he reported. "It's part of the Red Sea—divides Egypt and Jordan like the tip of a blade."

Simmons plugged the coordinates into a GPS device. "There's an old ruin there now. Looks totally abandoned."

Bumblebee slowed down as they came to a border checkpoint. Too late, Sam noticed a camera overhead, snapping a picture. The guard let them pass, but it was only a matter of time before they were found. Their location was no longer a secret.

"The whole world's gonna know we're here now," Sam realized. "We have to send a message to Lennox. Get him to bring Optimus to the Dagger's Tip."

Sam got the message to Major Lennox using Simmons's cell phone, hoping that it hadn't been traced. Bumblebee and the Twins stayed off of the main roads. By nighttime, they reached an abandoned tourist center near the three Pyramids of Giza. It was the perfect place to rest and come up with a plan.

Leo and Simmons slept inside one of the old wooden shacks. Sam and Mikaela sat on a bench, looking up at the stars. Sam kept thinking about Jetfire's translation of the symbols.

When Dawn alights the Dagger's Tip, Three Kings will reveal the doorway.

Thanks to Simmons, they knew about the Dagger's Tip. But the Three Kings?

Suddenly Sam jumped up. "The stars!" he cried.

Excited, Sam ran into the cabin. "Simmons, Leo, wake up! I know where the Three Kings are!"

They groggily followed Sam outside. He climbed onto the roof of the old tourist center and pointed. The stars shone above the three pyramids.

"Orion's Belt!" Sam cried. "Those three stars—they're also

called the Three Kings!"

He pointed to the pyramids. "Now look, the Pyramids of Giza—right under the three stars—built by three kings. It's like an arrow staring us right in the face."

"'Three Kings will reveal the doorway,'" Mikaela repeated. The pyramids faced a spot about fifty miles away, seeming to point at it.

"There!" Sam said with certainty. "That mountain ridge. The tomb's got to be over there."

They waited until just before dawn and then headed for the ridge. The ancient city of Petra was carved into red sandstone rock. A giant doorway loomed at the top of a long staircase.

As the sun rose, Sam climbed up the stairway into the city. Inside, the walls were covered with Roman murals. Soldiers in togas battled with swords. There were no alien symbols anywhere.

"What do we do now?" Leo asked.

CHAPTER 12

SAM WAS HOPEFUL. "IT'S GOT TO BE HERE SOMEWHERE. Everybody take a side of the room!"

They fanned out to search, but there was no sign of the Transformer tomb.

"Did it ever cross your mind that archaeologists have been here before?" Leo said snidely.

"This is not over," Sam said. "Everybody listen up!"

"We ain't listening to you, sucka," said the orange Twin. "What have you ever done for us?"

"He killed Megatron, how about that?" the green Twin shot back.

"Well, he didn't get the job done, 'cause Megatron's back!" said the orange Twin.

"What's the matter?" the green Twin asked. "You scared?"

The twins started pushing each other. The orange Twin crashed into the wall behind him, and a section of the Roman mural cracked off.

Underneath, the alien symbols gleamed.

Bumblebee broke away the rest of the mural. The symbols covered a section of metal ribbing in the wall.

"This is it!" Sam said, excited.

Bumblebee blasted through the metal to reveal the darkness of a tomb behind it. Sam was the first to step inside.

Sam gasped. The walls inside the tomb were made of the metal skeletons of twelve Transformers, their limbs fused together, just as Jetfire had said. One of the skeletons held a metal dagger with a crystal inside.

The Matrix of Leadership.

Sam reached for it. But before he could even touch it, the Matrix crumbled. A pile of black sand formed at Sam's feet.

"*No, no,* this is *not* how this ends!" Sam cried, panicking.

The sound of distant engines reached the tomb. Simmons rushed to the entrance.

"C-17s! Air Force! They're ours!" he shouted.

That meant Optimus was on the way—and Sam needed to get the Matrix to him, even if it had turned to dust. He took off his shoe and his sock, and then quickly filled the sock with the black sand.

"We didn't come here for nothing!" he cried. "The other Primes sacrificed their lives for this. Everyone's after me because of what I know, and what I know is—this is going to work."

"How do you know?" Mikaela asked him.

Sam looked into her eyes. "Because I believe it."

The planes landed at the old tourist center. Everyone hopped into Bumblebee. They had to get to Optimus—and fast.

They roared down the road, followed by the Twins. Suddenly Megatron and Starscream swooped down from the sky in jet form. The Twins zigzagged across the sand, sending clouds of dust into the air, causing the two Decepticons to lose visual contact with the Autobots. They circled back, ready for another strike.

Bumblebee ducked into an abandoned excavation site. The Twins pulled up beside him.

"We gotta split up," Sam said. "Bumblebee, you lead them away. I'll get to Optimus."

"Sir, yes, sir!" Bumblebee replied.

"Leo and I will help draw their fire with Huey and Dewey here," Simmons added. "You get to those soldiers. Hope that dust works, kid."

⫸ CHAPTER 13 ⫷

THE TWINS RACED ACROSS THE SAND AND FINALLY skidded to a stop in a deserted quarry. A pyramid towered above the pit.

"Megatron and Starscream aren't following us anymore," Leo said. "I don't think this worked."

Leo and Simmons climbed out of the green Twin and looked around. A dump truck and a green construction hauler hitched to a trailer were parked in the quarry. A cement mixer, an excavator, and a wheel loader came around the bend. On the ridge above them, a crane and a bulldozer rolled into view.

"Uh-oh," Simmons said. "Ever see that movie, *Gunfight at the O.K. Corral*?"

BOOM! A loud crack of thunder spun them around. The sky around the pyramid started to swirl. The swirling light formed a wormhole. Simmons and Leo watched, amazed, as a black Decepticon traveled through the hole and stood on top

of the pyramid—The Fallen. Megatron landed beside him.

"Master, your machine remains in place," Megatron told him in the Decepticon language.

"WHERE IS THE MATRIX?" The Fallen demanded.

The sound of creaking metal caused Leo and Simmons to turn away from the pyramid. The seven construction vehicles were joining together! The dump truck and the bulldozer formed two massive legs. The wheel loader and the crane became two enormous arms. The excavator and the hauler linked with the other parts to form a body and shoulders. The cement mixer linked up last, becoming a huge, helmeted head.

The new Decepticon, Devastator, was the biggest Transformer any of them had ever seen.

"We are in big trouble!" said the orange Twin.

Sam and Mikaela raced into an underground tunnel. A floor made of wooden slats rattled underneath their feet. The tunnel trembled as Starscream pounded the desert floor with missiles. Hearts thumping, they tore through the tunnel until it spit them out aboveground, right in the middle of the deserted tourist town. They were almost there!

BOOM! A Decepticon bulldozer slammed into the ground behind them. He chattered wildly in the language of the Decepticons. Sam glanced back and saw the 'bot's chest cavity open up. His parents were inside!

Sam and Mikaela stopped. The Decepticon dropped Ron and Judy onto the dirt. They looked roughed up but not hurt. The bulldozer aimed his arm cannon at them, shrieking.

Sam realized the 'bot was asking for a trade—his parents for the Matrix. What was he supposed to do?

WHAM! Just in time, Bumblebee flipped off the building, ninja-style, kicking the bulldozer to the ground. He pounded the Decepticon into pieces.

Ron and Judy ran to Sam and Mikaela. They all ducked into an alley.

"We've gotta move," Ron said. "Follow me!"

"No, Dad, they're after me," Sam said. "You get in Bumblebee. He'll get you out of here."

Ron and Judy didn't want to leave Sam behind, but they

realized Sam was right. They jumped into Bumblebee and sped away just as Megatron landed.

"I've searched the Earth for you, boy," Megatron said. "Today you die."

Megatron changed into a huge army tank and fired pulse blasts at the humans. Sam and Mikaela ran.

Over at the construction site, Devastator opened his huge mouth, creating an immense suction force. Leo and Simmons ran for cover as the giant swallowed everything in his path.

Devastator stomped toward the pyramid. He climbed to the top and started banging on the stone with his massive fist. He opened his mouth again, sucking up the broken pieces like a vacuum cleaner.

A twisting metal spire was revealed inside the pyramid. Simmons gasped.

"The machine—the machine that the plane was talking about," he said. "The pyramid is built right over it!"

⸺ CHAPTER 14 ⸺

TRUCKS CARRYING SOLDIERS SWARMED THE construction site. Helicopters overhead shot blasts at Devastator, but he just swatted at them like flies.

Simmons grabbed a radio from one of the soldiers. He contacted a navy ship as he ran toward the pyramid's base.

"Listen up!" he barked. "This is Agent Seymour Simmons, Sector Seven! Never heard of it? There's a reason. Now, do you want a throwdown about my lack of clearance, or do you want to save a gazillion lives?"

The naval commander knew he had no choice. Simmons asked him to aim a weapon called a rail gun at the pyramid to take down Devastator.

"I'll radio the exact coordinates in T-minus-five," Simmons said. Then he began his climb up to the top of the pyramid. He had to get there!

If the Decepticons got to that machine—then good-bye, sun!

Back in the desert town, Sam and Mikaela spotted Lennox and his men in the distance. A line of stone pillars stood between them and their goal. They ran from pillar to pillar, pursued by Megatron.

The abandoned town was a war zone now. Decepticons battled Autobots brought to the scene by Lennox and Epps. Military ships spilled marines and tanks onto the nearby beach to join the effort.

Through the smoke and haze, Lennox could see Sam and Mikaela crouching behind a pillar. Decepticons fired at them from all sides.

BAM! BAM! BAM! The marine tanks blasted the Decepticons, slowing them down. Lennox and Epps charged for Mikaela and Sam. They all dove into the sand as a pulse blast exploded overhead.

"Long time, no see," Lennox said. "Please tell me that you got what you came for."

"Where's Optimus?" Sam asked.

"Across the courtyard!" Lennox shouted over the blasts. "We make a break for the beach at my signal. We'll deal with him later. There's an air attack coming. It's the only way we'll ever get there. Stick with me—understand?"

Suddenly a Decepticon construction vehicle charged in front of them, blocking their path. Epps popped open cans that let off yellow smoke to hide their position. But the big machine plowed forward.

SLAM! Jetfire landed right on top of the Decepticon, blowing it to pieces.

"Darn young Decepticons today," Jetfire said. "No respect for a fair fight."

Suddenly Jetfire sustained a direct hit. He landed in the sand with a thud.

Overhead, four B-1 bombers flew over the town.

"When I give the word, do not stop running," Lennox ordered. "Go!"

Lennox took off across the courtyard as shrapnel rained all around them. Mikaela and Epps followed.

Sam veered to the right, heading for the beach. He had to get to Optimus!

Lennox and the others made it to cover just as the B-Is dropped a 2,000-pound bomb on the attacking Decepticons. The impact sent Sam into the dirt. He scrambled back to his feet and kept running.

But the bomb hadn't stopped Megatron. Still in tank form, he rolled through the black smoke until he reached Sam. Then he switched forms and aimed a pulse cannon at Sam.

BOOM! The blast hit a building right next to Sam, knocking him off his feet.

"The vendetta is paid!" Megatron exclaimed.

Then several Autobots and military vehicles quickly surrounded Megatron, forcing him to fly away. Mikaela ran up to Sam. He lay on the ground, still, with his eyes closed. The black dust spilled out of the sock next to Sam's body.

"Sam, wake up! Please wake up!" Mikaela pleaded.

But Sam didn't hear Mikaela. A bright white light flashed in his eyes. Sam stood up, staggering. The sand, the soldiers—everything was gone. All he could see was white light.

"Where am I?" Sam wondered.

The skeletons of Transformers materialized around him. They looked almost like ghosts with glowing eyes. The first one spoke.

"We are the Dynasty of the Primes," he said. "We have been watching you. For a long time."

"Watching me?" Sam asked.

"You do not yet know the full truth of your past," said the second Prime. "Nor of your future."

"I don't understand," Sam said.

"You will," promised the third Prime.

"You have fought for a Prime, our descendant. You have faced death for each other," said the fourth Prime.

The fifth Prime spoke. "Together, you are strong. Together, you will realize your destinies."

"For your sacrifice, your courage—virtues of a true leader—the Matrix of Leadership is yours," said the sixth Prime.

"But it's just dust," Sam said.

"Faith brought you this far," said the first Prime. "Don't lose it now."

A flash of energy blinded Sam. He opened his eyes. This time, he saw Mikaela, her eyes filled with tears.

"I love you, Sam," Mikaela sobbed. "Come back to me."

... CHAPTER 15 ...

SAM SAT UP. "I LOVE YOU, TOO."

Beside him the black sand swirled into the air, taking shape. Sam watched as the sand formed a black dagger with a crystal in the center—the Matrix of Leadership.

Sam grasped the dagger. He staggered over to Optimus and climbed up onto his chest. Then he plunged it into the center of the Transformer's chest.

The ancient symbols, all the old knowledge, passed from Sam into Optimus at that moment. The energy of the AllSpark shone from Optimus's core, glowing brighter each second. The Autobot slowly pulled himself to his knees.

"I knew there was greatness in you, Sam," he said.

"I'm sorry I didn't listen," Sam replied.

"But you did," Optimus assured him.

BAM!

The Fallen appeared before them in a flash. Ironhide and

Sideswipe charged at him, cannons firing. The Fallen swept his hands aside and sent them flying backward without even touching them. Next he aimed his force field at Optimus, slamming him back into the ground. He turned to Sam.

"So very many centuries . . . and your worthless race remains the same," The Fallen hissed.

Then he roared, sucking the Matrix right out of Sam's grasp.

"Revenge is mine," The Fallen said. "Now I claim your sun."

He quickly vanished, then appeared once more on top of the pyramid.

Still weak, Optimus tried to stand. "Autobots, stop him!"

Jetfire, still hurt from the attack, crawled up to him.

"Optimus, you are the last of the Primes," he said. "You possess powers beyond your own imagining. Take my parts and fulfill your destiny. All my life as a Decepticon, I never did a thing worth doing . . . until now."

The last glimmer of AllSpark inside Jetfire faded. He had sacrificed himself to give Optimus more energy. Grateful, Optimus quickly worked to remove Jetfire's wings and engine. When he finished, Optimus stood. Jetfire's sleek wings were fused to his back. He looked bigger and stronger than before.

BOOM! Optimus soared skyward, headed for the pyramid.

Devastator continued to break away the stone around the machine. Sweating and gasping, Simmons finally reached him. He called the naval destroyer again.

"Prepare to target your weapon!" he instructed. "I am directly below the enemy."

Above them, The Fallen placed the Matrix in the top spire of the machine as Megatron and Starscream looked on. Now it was aimed right at the sun.

Optimus flew in, roaring loudly, just as the navy's rail gun blasted Devastator in the chest. The gigantic Decepticon fell apart, tumbling to the sand below.

As Optimus soared up to the pyramid, a white beam shot

from the Matrix, powering up the machine.

SMASH! Optimus crashed into the tower. The lethal beam ricocheted wildly, striking Megatron, Starscream, and The Fallen. The Fallen charged at Optimus, eyes blazing.

"You dare challenge me? I AM A PRIME!"

The Fallen swept his hand, aiming a force field at Optimus. But Optimus held out his own hand, and a shimmering shield appeared, blocking The Fallen's attack.

"You abandoned that name when you slaughtered your brothers," Optimus said. "There is only one Prime now . . . and my ancestry will be avenged."

He leaped, wielding broken girders from the machine as weapons. His hands moved with lightning speed as he struck The Fallen and Megatron with powerful blows. Megatron cried out as his right arm flew off.

"You promised me, Master! You promised me the power of a Prime!" he yelled.

"Primes are born, not made," Optimus told him. "You were betrayed."

Optimus pummeled Megatron with the girders, smashing one of the Decepticon's legs. The Fallen opened a wormhole, trying to escape, but Optimus shot out a line of wire with sharp tethers on the end. The tethers gripped The Fallen, pulling him back.

"Megatron! Help me!" The Fallen cried.

But Megatron escaped into the wormhole, leaving his master behind.

The Fallen stared, unbelieving. Optimus grabbed the broken spike from the top of the machine. With incredible force, he drove it into The Fallen's skull.

The Fallen toppled off of the pyramid. Optimus grabbed the Matrix from inside the machine.

Then he flew across the desert sands, victorious.

··· CHAPTER 16 ···

SAM CLOSED HIS EYES AND SIGHED WITH RELIEF. EARTH was safe.

The remaining Decepticons quickly fled the scene. The green Twin carried an exhausted Simmons into the town. The orange Twin dragged Leo across the sand on a piece of metal.

Ron and Judy ran to Sam, hugging him.

When the reunion was over, they all boarded the navy battleship off the coast. Optimus and Sam stood on the ship's bow and looked out over the waves.

"The symbols in my head . . . they're gone," Sam said.

"Not gone," Optimus corrected him. "Part of my memory now."

Sam was quiet for a moment. "The Primes said we didn't know the truth about our future."

"I know one thing," Optimus replied. "It's a future we'll

meet together. Our planets. Our races. United by a history long forgotten, yet still to be discovered."

Sam nodded.

Whatever the future held, he knew now that he was ready for it.